Dragon's Extraordinary Egg

DEBI GLIORI

BLOOMSBURY

NEW YORK LONDON NEW DELHI SYDNEY

It's bedtime in the land of ice and snow.
"Night-night," says Bib's mommy.
"Sleep tight," says Bib's daddy.

But Bib has a better plan.
"Please . . . ," says Bib,
"can you read me a story?
The one about the dragons."

"Oh, Bib," sighs his mommy.
"Just one story, and then it's
night-night, sleep tight."

"Don't let the frost bite,"
says Bib, snuggling in.

Dragon's Extraordinary Egg

Long, long ago,
long before you hatched,
dragons came to live in our land of ice and snow.

They had lived all over the earth,
from east to west and all points in between,
but nowhere seemed just right.

So the dragons arrived in the icy vastness
of our land and set up camp.

"Did they have tents and sleeping bags
 in their camp?" asks Bib.
"I think they forgot to bring any," says Mommy.

So to keep warm they made their home
on top of a mountain with a fire in its heart,
and there they spent the long, long winter,
waiting for spring.

Sometimes it felt as if spring would never return,
but slowly the dark skies turned blue
and, drip by drip, the ice began to thaw.

At last, the sun returned to the frozen land.

The dragons loved the sun.
They stretched their long necks,
spread their wide wings,
and polished their hard, shiny scales.

Soon after that the eggs started coming.

Eggs with spots,
dots, and stripes.

Eggs with lumps,
bumps, and frills.

Some of the dragons laid little eggs.
Some of them laid **huge** ones.

But one dragon, with no egg at all,
went off to be alone for a while.

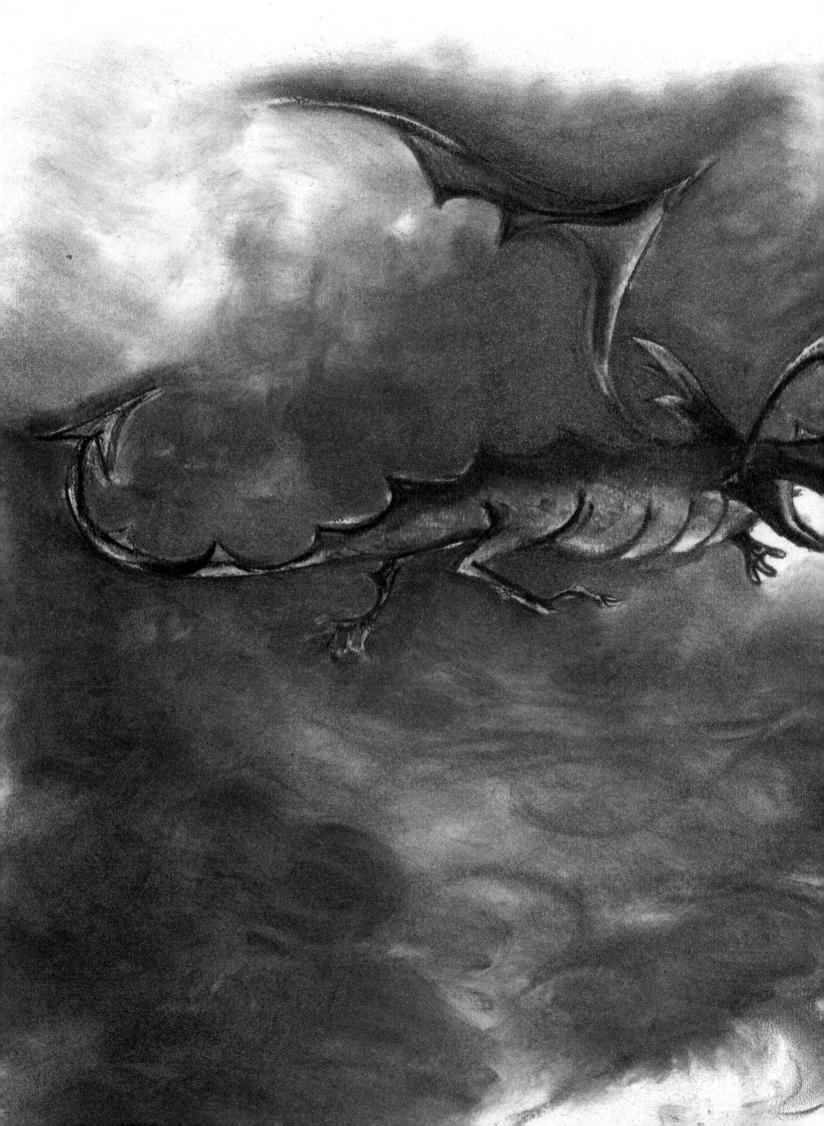

"Poor dragon," says Bib.
"I know," says Bib's mommy, "but . . .
sometimes things happen for a reason. Look."
"Oh!" gasps Bib. "Poor *egg*."

Yes, that egg needed
a mommy.

And that dragon
needed an egg.

It was a perfect fit.

The dragon loved her Little One
through ice and sun.

And through dark and dazzle,
Little One loved her back.

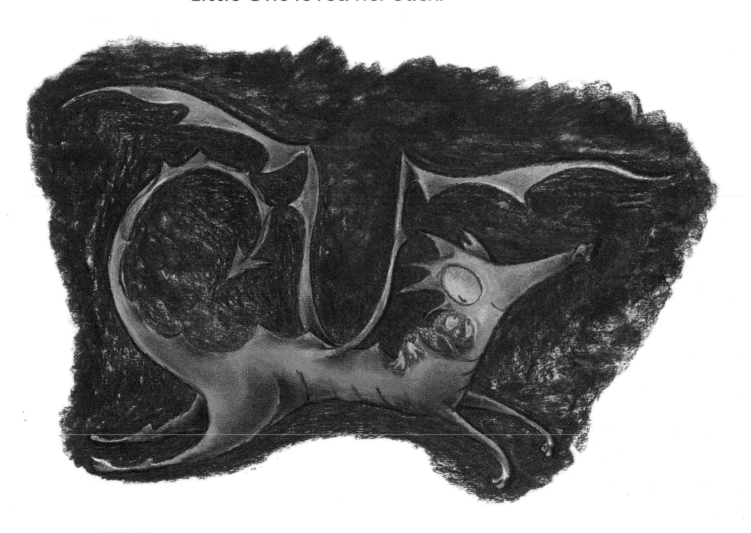

All the other eggs were
quick to learn . . .

how to fly . . .

and breathe fire . . .

and chew rocks.

But Little One
was slow and careful,
and learned to survive.

All the other eggs grew big and strong.
They grew long necks and wide wings
and hard scales all over.

But Little One, being small and fluffy,
grew courage instead.

All the other eggs were given endless gifts:
fast toys; vast toys; flashing,
clattering things that made a noise.
But Little One was given
love and time, the greatest gifts of all.

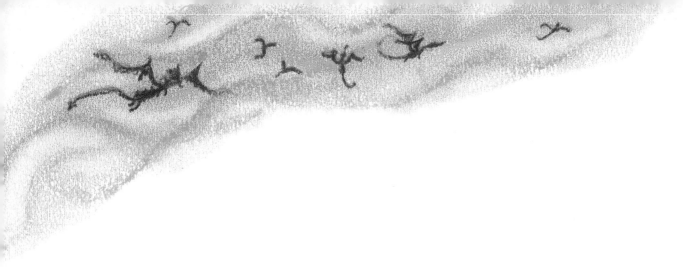

Then, one day, the big dragons had to go
far away to do big, important things.
Left behind, the small dragons grew scared and angry.
They picked fights with one another.
Then they turned on Little One.

"You're not a real dragon," they sneered. "You can't fly."
"You can't breathe fire."
"You're covered in feathers, you big . . . wimp."

"We're covered in feathers," says Bib.
"Yes," says Mommy. "Feathers keep us warm,
but they can't keep cold words out."

Feeling hurt and sad, Little One
went away to be alone for a while.

Sometimes things happen for a reason.

A real dragon's skin is too scaly to feel the heat,
but a soft, feathery dragon can feel the
first fiery breath when a volcano wakes up.

"FLEE FOR YOUR LIVES!" Little One screamed.
"THE MOUNTAIN IS ALIVE!"

The small dragons didn't wait to be told twice.
They didn't wait for Little One either.

Little One tried to fly, but her wings were too small.

She tried to run, but the flames ran too fast.

She screamed for help, but the roaring fire was too loud.

Then she fell over, onto her soft,
feathery tummy.

Which was exactly
the right thing to do . . .

Sometimes things happen
for a reason.

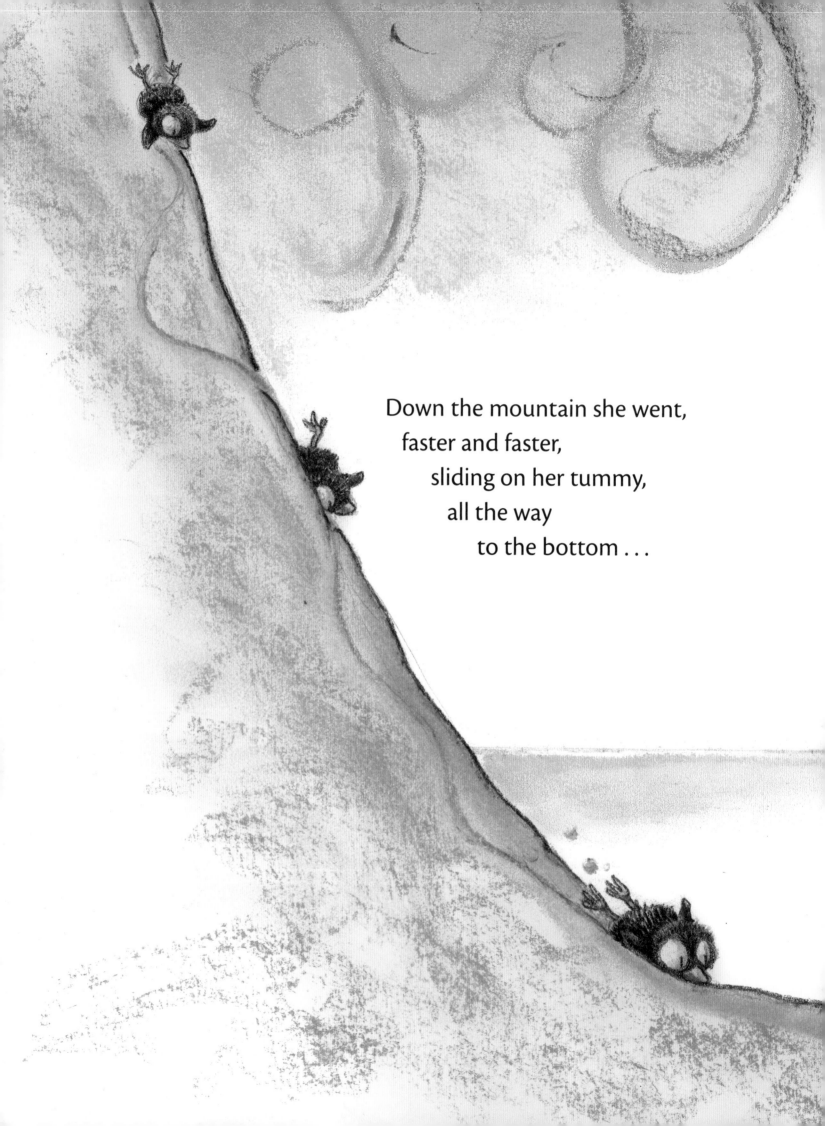

Down the mountain she went,
faster and faster,
sliding on her tummy,
all the way
to the bottom . . .

. . . where she found something waiting for her.

An egg!

The egg was very small,
but Little One had more
than enough courage for
both of them.

And thanks to her mommy,
Little One knew how to
survive through days of dark
and dazzle and ice and sun.

And much later, when the
egg hatched, who do you
think was inside?

"ME!" squeaks Bib.
"YOU!" says Mommy.

"I was the egg and
you were Little One!"
says Bib.
"YES," says Mommy.

"And I knew the best gift to give you. Love and time. Just like my dragon mommy gave me. And now it's time to snuggle down—"

"Read it again," says Bib. "Please?"

"Maybe Grandma will tell you the story this time," says Mommy.

"Please, please, please," says Bib.
"The dragon one. About you, and
mommy, and me?"

"Snuggle down," says Grandma.
"Close your eyes and I'll begin."

Long, long ago,
long before you hatched . . .

For my Dragons, with love —DG

First published as *Dragon Loves Penguin* in Great Britain in 2013 by Bloomsbury Publishing Plc
Published in the United States of America in October 2014 by Bloomsbury Children's Books
www.bloomsbury.com

Bloomsbury is a registered trademark of Bloomsbury Publishing Plc

For information about permission to reproduce selections from this book, write to Permissions, Bloomsbury Children's Books, 1385 Broadway, New York, New York 10018
Bloomsbury books may be purchased for business or promotional use. For information on bulk purchases please contact
Macmillan Corporate and Premium Sales Department at specialmarkets@macmillan.com

Library of Congress Cataloging-in-Publication Data
available upon request
ISBN 978-0-8027-3759-5 (hardcover)
ISBN 978-0-8027-3767-0 (e-book) • ISBN 978-0-8027-3768-7 (e-PDF)

Printed in China by C&C Offset Printing Co Ltd, Shenzhen, Guangdong
2 4 6 8 10 9 7 5 3 1

All papers used by Bloomsbury Publishing, Inc., are natural, recyclable products made from wood grown in well-managed forests.
The manufacturing processes conform to the environmental regulations of the country of origin.